CW00455173

# A CHILD'S DREAM

## OF A STAR.

Copyright © 2020 Read & Co. Books

This edition is published by Read & Co. Books,
an imprint of Read & Co.

This book is copyright and may not be reproduced or copied in any
way without the express permission of the publisher in writing.

British Library Cataloguing-in-Publication Data
A catalogue record for this book is available
from the British Library.

Read & Co. is part of Read Books Ltd.
For more information visit
www.readandcobooks.co.uk

# A CHILD'S DREAM

OF

# A STAR.

### By CHARLES DICKENS.

*WITH ILLUSTRATIONS BY HAMMATT BILLINGS.*

# LIST OF ILLUSTRATIONS.

ENGRAVED BY W. J. LINTON.

# A CHILD'S
# DREAM OF A STAR.

HERE was once a child, and he strolled about a good deal, and thought of a number of things. He had a sister, who was a child too, and his constant companion. These two used to wonder all day long. They wondered at the beauty of the flowers; they wondered at the height and blueness of the sky; they wondered at the depth of the bright water; they wondered at

the goodness and the power of GOD, who made the lovely world.

They used to say to one another, sometimes, Supposing all the children upon earth were to die, would the flowers and the water and the sky be sorry? They believed they would be sorry. For, said they, the buds are the children of the flowers, and the little playful streams that gambol down the hillsides are the children of the water; and the smallest bright specks playing at hide-and-seek in the sky all night must surely be the children of the stars; and they would all be grieved to see their playmates, the children of men, no more.

There was one clear shining star that used to come out in the sky before the

rest, near the church-spire, above the graves. It was larger and more beautiful, they thought, than all the others, and every night they watched for it, standing hand in hand at a window. Whoever saw it first cried out, " I see the star ! " And often they cried out both together, knowing so well when it would rise and where. So they grew to be such friends with it, that, before lying down in their beds, they always looked out once again, to bid it good night; and when they were turning round to sleep, they used to say, " God bless the star ! "

But while she was still very young, O, very, very young, the sister drooped, and came to be so weak that she could no longer stand in the window at night; and

then the child looked sadly out by himself, and when he saw the star, turned round and said to the patient pale face on the bed, " I see the star ! " And then a smile would come upon the face, and a little weak voice used to say, " God bless my brother and the star ! "

And so the time came, all too soon ! when the child looked out alone, and when there was no face on the bed; and when there was a little grave among the graves, not there before ; and when the star made long rays down towards him, as he saw it through his tears.

Now, these rays were so bright, and they seemed to make such a shining way from earth to heaven, that when the child went to his solitary bed, he dreamed about

the star; and dreamed that, lying where he was, he saw a train of people taken up that sparkling road by angels. And the star, opening, showed him a great world of light, where many more such angels waited to receive them.

All these angels, who were waiting, turned their beaming eyes upon the people who were carried up into the star; and some came out from the long rows in which they stood, and fell upon the people's necks, and kissed them tenderly, and went away with them down avenues of light, and were so happy in their company, that, lying in his bed, he wept for joy.

But there were many angels who did not go with them, and among them one

he knew. The patient face that once had lain upon the bed was glorified and radiant, but his heart found out his sister among all the host.

His sister's angel lingered near the entrance of the star, and said to the leader among those who had brought the people thither, " Is my brother come? "

And he said, " No."

She was turning hopefully away, when the child stretched out his arms, and cried, " O sister, I am here! Take me! " And then she turned her beaming eyes upon him, and it was night; and the star was shining into the room, making long rays down towards him as he saw it through his tears.

From that hour forth, the child looked

out upon the star as on the home he was to go to, when his time should come; and he thought that he did not belong to the earth alone, but to the star too, because of his sister's angel gone before.

There was a baby born to be a brother to the child; and while he was so little that he never yet had spoken word, he stretched his tiny form out on his bed, and died.

Again the child dreamed of the opened star, and of the company of angels, and the train of people, and the rows of angels with their beaming eyes all turned upon those people's faces.

Said his sister's angel to the leader, "Is my brother come?"

And he said, "Not that one, but another."

As the child beheld his brother's angel in her arms, he cried, "O sister, I am here! Take me!" And she turned and smiled upon him, and the star was shining.

He grew to be a young man, and was busy at his books when an old servant came to him and said, "Thy mother is no more. I bring her blessing on her darling son!"

Again at night he saw the star, and all that former company. Said his sister's angel to the leader, "Is my brother come?"

And he said, "Thy mother!"

A mighty cry of joy went forth through

all the star, because the mother was re-
united to her two children. And he
stretched out his arms and cried, "O
mother, sister, and brother, I am here!
Take me!"

And they answered him, "Not yet."
And the star was shining.

He grew to be a man, whose hair was
turning gray; and he was sitting in his
chair by the fireside, heavy with grief,
and with his face bedewed with tears,
when the star opened once again.

Said his sister's angel to the leader,
"Is my brother come?"

And he said, "Nay, but his maiden
daughter."

And the man who had been the child
saw his daughter, newly lost to him, a

celestial creature among those three, and he said, "My daughter's head is on my sister's bosom, and her arm is round my mother's neck, and at her feet there is the baby of old time, and I can bear the parting from her, GOD be praised!"

And the star was shining.

Thus the child came to be an old man, and his once smooth face was wrinkled, and his steps were slow and feeble, and his back was bent. And one night as he lay upon his bed, his children standing round, he cried, as he had cried so long ago, "I see the star!"

They whispered one another, "He is dying."

And he said, "I am. My age is falling from me like a garment, and I move

towards the star as a child. And O my Father, now I thank thee that it has so often opened to receive those dear ones who await me!"

And the star was shining; and it shines upon his grave.

15

Printed in Great Britain
by Amazon

58124465R00017